D0123045

Hiking the trails in Piedmont Park

The English Roses

American Dreams

CALLAWAY ARTS & ENTERTAINMENT
19 FULTON STREET, FIFTH FLOOR, NEW YORK, NEW YORK 10038

PUFFIN BOOKS
Published by the Penguin Group
Penguin Young Readers Group, 345 Hudson Street, New York, New York 10014, U.S.A.
Penguin Group (Canada), 90 Eglinton Avenue East, Suite 700, Toronto, Ontario,
Canada M4P2Y3 (a division of Pearson Penguin Canada Inc.)

Penguin Books Ltd., Registered Offices: 80 Strand, London WC2R 0RL, England

First published in the United States of America by Callaway Arts & Entertainment and Puffin Books, 2009

1 3 5 7 9 10 8 6 4 2

First Edition

Produced by Callaway Arts & Entertainment
Nicholas Callaway, President and Publisher
John Lee, CEO
Cathy Ferrara, Managing Editor and Production Director
Toshiya Masuda, Art Director
Nelson Gómez, Director of Digital Technology
Amy Cloud, Senior Editor
Bomina Kim, Design Assistant
Ivan Wong, Jr. and José Rodríguez, Production
Jennifer Caffrey, Executive Assistant

Special thanks to Doug Whiteman and Mariann Donato.

Library of Congress Cataloging-in-Publication Data is available.

Puffin Books ISBN 978-0-14-241128-5

Printed in the United States of America

www.madonna.com www.callaway.com www.penguin.com/youngreaders

All of Madonna's proceeds from this book will be donated to
Raising Malawi (www.raisingmalawi.org), an orphan-care initiative.

The English Roses
by MADONNA
With Rebecca Gómez
American Dreams
illustrated by jeffrey fulvimari
PUFFIN
CALLAWAY
New York
2009
Book 11

Contents

CHAPTER I

Consider All the Angles

I could just begin right here. No one would blame me, I'm sure, if I made certain assumptions about you, dear reader. I am quite sure that you are simply saturated with English Roses fabulosity. You're so up on all things E.R. (that's short for "English Roses," don'cha know?) that you're ahead of all of us. I won't do that, though. Nope, that's not how I'm playing. Why, you ask? Well, although you and I are on the same page, there may exist a reader somewhere who is not quite as intimately acquainted with the English Roses as we. Hard to imagine, I know. But as Miss Fluffernutter (the girls' ab fave teacher) is so fond of saying, we must "consider all the angles."

Maybe you yourself are not clear on this whole English Roses phenomenon. Perhaps you have been away. Let's say you've just been released from an asylum for the criminally insane. If so, please move a bit away from me. Thank you. So you see, don't you, why I can't just jump into our story feet-first? It simply wouldn't be fair. For those of you who do need a bit of background, here's what the English Roses are not:

1. Astral projections
2. Albino goldfish
3. Dwarf cacti

astral projections? NO.

albino goldfish? NO.

dwarf cacti? DOUBLE NO.

The English Roses are a group of five friends, although a simple word like "friends" doesn't begin to do them justice. Five fast friends—Amy Brook, Grace Harrison, Binah Rossi, Charlotte Ginsberg, and Nicole Rissman—are students at Hampstead School in London. The English Roses give one another fashion advice, romance tips, homework help, and anything else for which friends might be called upon. More than that, the English Roses love one another. They celebrate happy occasions together and offer support for the not-so-happy times. They are one another's cheerleaders and confidantes and shoulders-to-cry-on. There is nothing they wouldn't do for one another. Nothing.

Don't get the wrong idea here. The English Roses are not clones. They're not exactly alike.

Each is from a very different family and circumstances. And that's the beauty of it: Together they add up to more than the sum of their parts!

What happens when such a tightly knit group is separated by that most wondrous of events: summer vacation? What do you think? Read on to find out.

CHAPTER 2

Sand in Your Smoothie

Have you ever been completely and utterly disappointed by something but still try to convince everyone (in this case, your four best friends) that you're not? That it's really no big deal because you don't want them to feel sorry for you? Am I making any sense here? Whoops! There I go again, getting ahead of myself. It's life we're talking about here. Things are moving along smoothly and then it's as if someone threw a pound of sand into your fruit smoothie!

The Roses were exactly where you'd expect to find them on this late-May Saturday morning: at the park, under their favorite tree. Nicole was tracing leaves in a journal, working on some science project, no doubt! Amy's pencil danced over her sketch pad as she tried to capture some ducks in flight.

"Darn it!" She sighed, crumpling up a sheet of paper. She tossed it into the growing pile next to her.

"What's up, Amy?" Grace asked as she repeatedly headed a football (what you Yanks call a soccer ball) against the tree trunk. Her aim was frighteningly good!

Amy flipped her pad to a fresh page. "I just can't get the angle the way I want it. Maybe I should stick to fashion sketches."

"You never know where your inspiration will come from," Binah chimed in, looking up from her knitting. "Maybe your breakthrough creation will have ducks in flight on it!"

Charlotte laughed. "That sounds more like a sleeping bag, Binah!"

As all the Roses laughed at that, Charlotte started unpacking the picnic hamper at her feet.

"Who's hungry?" she asked. "Nigella has packed

us all sorts of yummy treats!" (Okay, assuming you are one of those readers who's just been released from a home for the criminally insane, you need to know that Nigella is Charlotte's family's chef. Yes, family chef. I'm well aware of how that sounds. Let's just say that Charlotte's family has more . . . disposable income than most. The other Roses deal with it; they love to tease Charlotte on occasion, but they're also happy to get rides from the Ginsbergs' driver and eat the scrumptious food Nigella makes. So I suggest that you deal with it, too!)

"Me!" cried Grace.

"You're always hungry, Grace!" Binah teased her friend.

"I can't help it," Grace defended herself sheepishly.

"Grace," Nicole said, "if we were all half as active as you, we'd eat a lot more, too!"

"I just love food," Grace continued, giving Nicole a grateful smile. "As I was jogging over here this morning, I was thinking about all the foods that I love. The one reason I'm looking forward to vacation is going back to the U.S. My aunt's barbeques are not to be believed!"

"The one reason?" Amy asked.

"Well," Grace answered, "I'm not looking forward to not being with the four of you. But I do love to visit my family in Atlanta."

"Where are we all going to be?" Charlotte asked,

pulling out her sleek leather address book. "I need to know how to get in touch with each of you. The break is such a long time. Two weeks without you all will be so hard!"

"I'll be in Georgia!" sang Grace.

"We're heading to our little villa in the south of France," Charlotte stated. (Yes, you read correctly; the Ginsbergs also have a home in France. Let it go; don't be a hater!)

"Nicole and I will be in Wales for two weeks," Amy said.

"I can't wait!" Nicole added. "We're going to this awesome creative arts camp! I'm going to study scientific illustration and modern dance."

"I am *so* not studying scientific illustration," Amy said. "But I am going to take drawing classes and sculpture classes and some performing arts and dance. . . ." She trailed off with a sigh and a smile, clearly looking forward to camp.

"Binah," Charlotte prompted, "are we all coming back to London at the same time? You are going to be at your grandmother's house, right? I want to double check her address. It's no fun sending postcards if I'm not sure you'll receive them!"

Binah was quiet for a moment.

"Binah?" Grace asked.

"Are you going to your nonna's?" Amy asked her.

Binah cleared her throat and looked intently at the knitting she held in her hands. "Ummm, not exactly."

"What do you mean, 'not exactly'?" Grace queried.

Nicole gazed at Binah with concern. "What's going on, Binah?"

To her horror, Binah felt tears welling up in her eyes. She cleared her throat again and blinked rapidly to clear up those stupid tears. She took a deep breath and gazed around the circle at her beloved friends. They deserved an explanation. What's more, they weren't going to let her get away without spilling her guts. Might as well get it over with!

"There's been a slight change of plans," Binah started. She was very happy to hear that her voice came out clear and strong. There was no hint of the sadness threatening to make her voice crack.

"What?" Grace asked.

"Well," Binah continued, "my Nonna Rossi is going to Scotland with her senior citizens' group. They're going to stay at a castle and see all kinds of brill things and eat interesting food and hear lectures. It's going to be a blast!"

"For Nonna Rossi," Charlotte said flatly.

"What about Binah?" Nicole asked gently.

"I'm going to be fine," Binah told them. "I've got all sorts of plans cooked up. I'm going to work on my knitting and refinish a bureau and take long walks and catch up on my reading."

"What?!" Grace asked again, incredulously.

"Binah," Nicole said, "that's no vacation plan!"

"It's perfect," Binah said firmly. "I will have a great break. My dad and I will do fun things. I'll miss you all, but it will be great to catch up when you get back!" (Here's the 411 on Binah: Her mum died when Binah was just a little girl. She lives with her dad, who works as a carpenter. They don't have pots of money, but both Binah and her father work hard to have the things they need. Binah is, as Miss Fluffernutter has said, an old soul. She is wise and kind and unselfish. Sometimes too unselfish, if you ask the rest of the Roses.)

BINAH'S KNITTING

Silence descended on all of the Roses. This is a rare occurrence, I can assure you! It was awkward for a moment: Each of the other Roses thought about her extravagant summer plans. Binah smiled at each of them, willing them not to feel sorry for her. Yes, there was sand in her smoothie, but it was *her* smoothie; she didn't want to bring her friends down. It wasn't working; the others could read her like a book. Hey, these are inseparable best friends, you know!

Finally, Charlotte broke the silence. "Who's hungry?" she asked. "Nigella will be awfully upset if I bring any food home!"

"We don't want to upset Nigella." Grace laughed. "Load me up a plate, Charlotte!"

"I'm hungry, too!" Binah cried.

"Let's eat!" Nicole said.

As they munched on their snacks, Binah brought up the subject again, determined to allay her friends' fears. "I'll learn some new recipes while you're gone," she promised. "I want you all to send me lots of postcards and promise to have a great time."

"You're too much, Binah!" Grace said.

And she was right.

CHAPTER 3

The Big Idea

If you know anything about the English Roses, and I suspect you do, you must realize that they have a very keen sense of injustice. And Binah's vacation plans simply didn't seem fair to the other Roses. Believe you me, the phone lines linking Charlotte, Amy, Grace, and Nicole were crackling that night! Try as they might,

though, no one could come up with a good plan for Binah. What to do?

Monday morning found the girls back at Hampstead School. Although summer vacation loomed in every student's mind, it hadn't quite arrived; and that meant business as usual. Which is, in a way, fortunate, because that led to the Big Idea. Whoops! There I go again, getting too far ahead of myself. Didn't I ask you to stop me when I do that?

The morning unfolded uneventfully. The Roses met, as usual, in the cafeteria to have lunch together. It was such a beautiful afternoon that students were allowed to eat their lunches outside near the football field.

"Why is the caf so crowded?" Charlotte complained.

"I don't know, but I don't need to pick up anything," Binah said. "So I'll go out and find us a good spot."

"I'm coming with you, Binah," said Grace. "It's a zoo in here!"

Binah and Grace headed outside and found a lovely, quiet spot in a corner of the courtyard. When Nicole, Charlotte, and Amy joined them, they had an explanation for the overcrowded caf.

"It's the Book Exchange!" Nicole exclaimed. "It's one of my favorite events."

"Why do you like it so much?" Grace asked as she munched on her sandwich and kicked a foot idly.

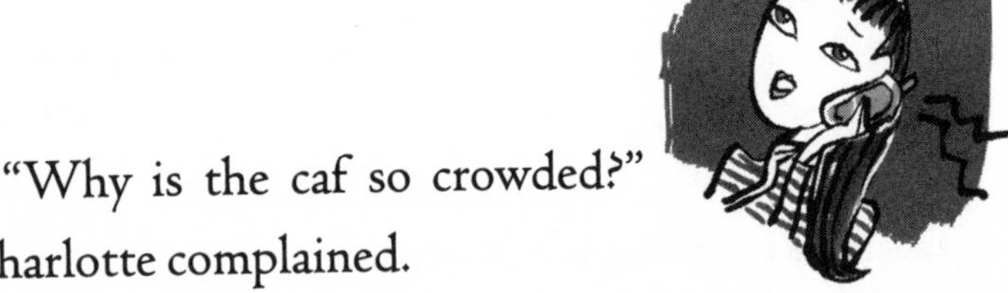

"Are you kidding?" Charlotte asked. "Why does Nicole like the Book Exchange?"

"Don't tease me!" Nicole protested, although she knew her friends were joking. "I get all my summer reading at the Book Exchange, every year, without fail."

"Summer reading?" Charlotte asked. "Yuck!"

"No, it's great," Nicole answered. "I bring in all the old books I've already read and get to pick an equal number of new books. It's fantastic!"

"Only you, Nicole." Amy laughed. "Only you would get so excited about the idea of new books."

"I've picked up some good books, too," Binah said.

"It's also great for the environment," Amy added. "We're recycling!"

"Hooray for us!" Charlotte giggled.

"Hmm," Grace mumbled.

"You've been awfully quiet, Grace," Charlotte noted. "You don't *have* to pick books, you know!"

Suddenly, Grace jumped to her feet, spilling her water bottle and not even seeming to notice. "I've got it!" she cried.

"You've got what?" Amy asked.

"I've got the answer to our summer vacation problem!" she said.

"What problem?" Binah asked, looking at her friends curiously.

The other Roses looked at one another guiltily.

"Oh, Binah—" Nicole started.

Amy interrupted her. "Binah, we couldn't stand it that you were going to be here all summer, alone!"

Grace tried to speak. "Here's what I'm thinking—"

"It's not fair," Charlotte continued. "We are all going on these fab trips, and you're going to be here."

"But I'll be fine!" Binah protested.

"We know you'll be fine," Nicole rushed in. "We don't feel sorry for you, please believe me. We just want you to have fun, too."

"If I can explain—" Grace tried to interject.

"But I will have fun!" Binah insisted.

"We know," Amy said, "but we've been trying to think of something really great for you."

"Quiet!" Grace roared, startling all of the Roses . . . and some of their classmates seated nearby, too.

"Sorry, Grace," Nicole said.

"What's your idea?" Charlotte asked.

"Yeah, fill us in!" said Amy.

Binah said nothing but twisted her napkin nervously in her hands. In her heart of hearts, she wished she had exciting vacation plans, too. But she would never tell the others that.

"It's perfect," said Grace. "Actually, the Book Exchange gave me the idea!"

"Well?" Nicole said.

"And to think," Grace continued, "I don't even *like* the Book Exchange!"

"Grace!" Charlotte almost shouted. "What's your idea??"

"Oh yes," Grace answered. "I must say, it's my best idea ever! Binah needs summer plans, right?"

"Don't say a word, Binah," Nicole warned her friend, but gave her a big hug.

"I fly back and forth to Atlanta every summer," Grace said. "Guess what I get on every trip?"

"Souvenirs?" guessed Charlotte.

"Jet lag?" joked Amy.

"No, seriously, guys!" Grace said. "I collect frequent-flier miles every time I fly. I must have gadzillions of them by now."

"That is brill, Grace," Charlotte the world traveler caught on. "You can redeem your frequent-flier miles for a ticket for Binah!"

Having tons of fun in the Atlanta sun

"My family would love to have Binah visit," Grace said. "My aunt always asks me when I'm bringing my London friends back to Atlanta. I hope you know that you all have a standing invitation."

Binah was quiet, but a smile was growing on her face.

"It's perfect!" Nicole agreed. "No one will have to pay for airfare, and Binah will have a nice place to stay."

"You'll love Atlanta!" Grace told Binah, who by now had a huge grin plastered across her face.

"I was going to ask you what you think of the idea," Amy said to Binah. "But I think your thoughts are obvious!"

Binah took a deep breath.

"Well, Bee?" Nicole said.

"It's very generous of you, Grace," Binah began. She almost couldn't let herself believe her good fortune. "But are you sure your parents will be okay with it? Don't they want to use the miles for something else?"

"With all five of us flying back and forth at least once a year," Grace said, "we've earned more miles than we could ever spend. Plus, my parents take other trips without Matthew, Michael, and me. We'll never redeem them all!"

"It sounds like so much fun," Binah said. "Thank you, Grace. If it's okay with my dad, I would absolutely love to go to Atlanta this summer!"

"We'll have a blast!" Grace told them. And they all nodded their heads, very pleased with themselves. Because, after all, who knew?

CHAPTER 4

It's a Bird, It's a Plane, It's Binah!

Were airplanes always this noisy, Binah wondered? She just didn't know; this was her first flight. Their plane was sitting on the runway, awaiting takeoff instructions (at least, according to the announcement the pilot had just made). It seemed to Binah that a million conversations were going on at once, several children were wailing, and the man next to her had his headphone volume turned very high. Even over the din of the cabin, Binah could hear the tinny sounds escaping from his ear buds. Grace was next to her, looking out the window.

"So long, London," Grace said, then smiled at Binah. Binah smiled back, unwilling to admit to Grace, or to herself, just how nervous she was. *How do airplanes work?* she wondered. She wished she'd paid closer attention during science class!

For Binah, the last few weeks of school had flown by in a blur of activity. Grace's parents had been thrilled by Grace's plan. They were always happy for Grace to have female company, surrounded as she usually was by her twin older brothers. As Binah suspected he would, Mr. Rossi had given his approval for her trip, too. He knew that his daughter would be well looked after by the Harrisons. More than that, he knew that Binah would be happy, truly happy, with her friend. As a dad, what more could he ask?

Nonna Rossi had been very exicted about Binah's trip, too. She had felt badly that she was leaving Binah behind for her trip to Scotland. Now she could go off with her senior citizens' group and not worry. Just before she left for Scotland, she'd stopped by to see Mr. Rossi and Binah. Nonna Rossi had been to the United States many years ago, and she told Binah stories of her adventures. When she left, she'd taken an envelope out of her purse. Handing it to Binah she said, "It's not as much as I would like to give you, Binah, but at least it will get you started."

"Oh, Nonna!" Binah cried. "What is this?"

"Open it and see!" her grandmother said.

Binah slit the envelope and found five crisp twenty-dollar bills inside. "Is this real money?" she

asked. "It looks so funny!"

Nonna Rossi laughed. "Yes, Binah. I exchanged some money at the bank. It's one hundred American dollars."

"Thank you, Nonna!" Binah said, giving her grandmother a huge hug.

"My pleasure, sweetie," Nonna Rossi answered. "I want you to go and enjoy yourself. Have the time of your life!"

Now Binah reached into her backpack and felt for the money. She'd tucked it into her wallet, along with the money she herself had saved. Papa had given her some money, too. In total, she had

$250 in her purse. Even though the money didn't feel real, Binah felt like the queen!

Adding to her sense of luxury was her new backpack, a present from the Roses. The other three had chipped in to buy Binah and Grace matching backpacks. Binah loved her cherry pink backpack, which had her name stitched across the top in flowing navy script. Grace's rucksack was a no-nonsense black, and her name appeared in chunky white letters. "To each her own!" Nicole had said when she handed them over. Binah and Grace had been touched to find the packs already stuffed with magazines, chewing gum, slipper socks, and pre-addressed postcards. "Everything you'll need for a successful flight," Charlotte had assured them both breezily.

Binah thought about the other Roses. She and Grace were about to lift off. Charlotte had left yesterday for her family's drive to the south of France. Nicole and Amy were scheduled to leave for Wales tomorrow. Binah wondered how London would fare without an English Rose in sight for a whole two weeks! To quell her nerves, she popped a piece of gum in her mouth, closed her eyes, and imagined what her papa was doing at that very instant. She missed him already!

Just then, the pilot asked the flight attendants to prepare for takeoff and the jet engines screamed to life. Binah almost swallowed her gum as she was thrust back into her seat when the plane began racing down the runway. She looked at Grace again, but Grace was back to looking out the window.

Here goes nothing! Binah thought as the plane bumped once and then gently lifted into the sky. Binah felt her stomach give a disconcerting twinge and then began to feel completely disoriented as one wing dipped and London was spread out below Grace's window.

"It's so beautiful!" Grace cried.

Binah agreed, but couldn't make herself look out the window for very long. She concentrated on the seat back in front of her as she waited for the plane to level off . . . as Charlotte had assured her it would.

"It feels strange in the beginning," Charlotte had cautioned. "But you'll get used to it. I love to fly!"

Binah wondered about that.

She was still wondering more than two hours

later when the plane, which had been moving smoothly through the air, started to shake. The pilot's announcement that they were encountering a little turbulence woke Binah from a semislumber. Grace's head was slumped against the window and she was snoring gently. The man next to Binah had finally turned off his headphones and he, too, appeared to be sleeping. *What's turbulence?* Binah wondered.

Suddenly, the plane started to dip and buck. Binah gripped her armrests until her knuckles were white. Grace started from her sleep and looked at Binah in confusion.

"What's going on?" she asked.

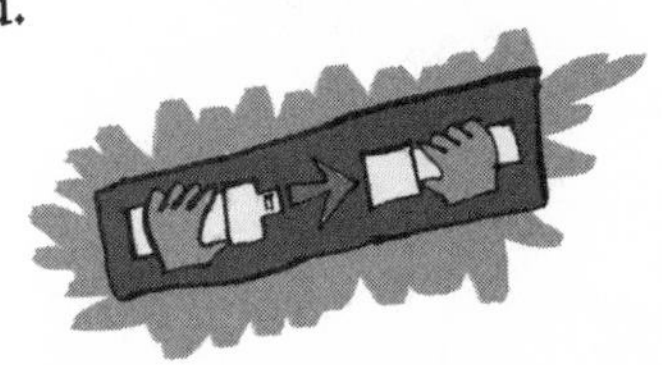

"The pilot just made an announcement about turbulence. I guess this is turbulence!" Binah couldn't help a small cry from escaping her mouth. Were they crashing?

Grace gave a giggle, shocking Binah.

"Ooooh!" she said. "I love turbulence."

"You what?" Binah said. She couldn't believe her ears.

"Turbulence is like a fab roller coaster. Just ride it out!" Grace urged.

"But I hate roller coasters!" Binah whispered.

Somewhere near the back of the plane a baby had woken and started to cry. Binah felt like crying herself. Then she, ominously, felt something else. Her stomach, which had felt a little flippy during takeoff, gave a lurch.

"Grace . . ." she started.

Grace took one look at her friend's pale face and immediately grabbed an airsickness bag from the pocket of the seat back in front of her. "Use this!" she told Binah.

Almost before she knew it, Binah was vomiting into the little white, waxy bag. She hadn't had much to eat, but her stomach kept heaving, and the most horrible sounds were coming out of her. Binah was sure the whole plane could hear her, especially Michael and Matthew, seated several rows behind her. She even woke the man seated next to her. Binah noticed his sympathetic look once when she came up for air. Somehow, it didn't help.

Grace was rubbing her back and making little clucking noises.

AIR SICK-NESS BAG

"It's okay, Binah," she said.

"Ugh!" was all that Binah could say in response.

"Do you want me to get my mom?" Grace asked.

"No! Please, no," Binah said desperately.

Just then the unfasten seatbelt light pinged on overhead. The pilot came back over the intercom, assuring them that they were through the turbulence. The plane resumed its smooth trajectory through the sky.

Grace handed Binah some tissues. "You can use these to wipe your mouth," she said.

"Thanks, Grace," Binah said shakily. "I feel better now. What should I do with this bag?" She wrinkled her nose at the offending object.

"I can bring it back to the bathroom for you," Grace offered.

"No, I'll do it," Binah said. "Do you think it's safe to walk around now?"

"Absolutely," Grace said. "Don't feel badly, Binah. My little cousins throw up on planes all the time."

Somehow Grace's words, meant so kindly, only added to Binah's misery. And then, to add insult to injury, she had to pass the rest of the Harrisons on her way back to the lav. She tried to smile brightly at them. "I'm having a great trip!" was her answer to their question.

Great, she thought as she shut the bathroom door behind her, sliding the little latch into place. *Now I'm a liar as well as a lousy traveler!*

She gave herself a little shake as she started back to her seat. "No problem," Binah said to herself. "I'm just lucky to be on this trip. Soon enough we'll be on the ground, and I'll be in the United States!"

She repeated this over and over again. She repeated it throughout their landing, hours later, as the plane dropped and her stomach lurched.

i'm lucky to
be on this TRIP
i'm lucky to
be on this TRIP
i'm lucky to
be on this TRIP

(Fortunately, she didn't have to use another of the little white bags!) She repeated it as her ears rang and popped. She repeated it as the runway rushed up at the plane and they bounced once, then again, as they landed. Then they were down and the passengers started clapping.

"Wasn't that fun?" Grace asked Binah. "We're finally here!"

"Yes, sure," Binah said. She didn't sound very convincing to herself, but Grace didn't seem to notice. As the plane taxied to their gate, she and Grace gathered up their belongings.

"Welcome to the United States of America, Binah!" Grace cried as she hugged her friend.

"Thanks, Grace!" Binah said. *Here goes nothing!* she thought.

Welcome to the U.S. of A....
ATLANTA INTERNATIONAL AIRPORT
BRITISH AIRWAYS

CHAPTER 5

Sweet Home Atlanta

The first thing that struck Binah about Atlanta was the size of Grace's family. It seemed that the whole city of Atlanta had turned up at the airport to meet them. Grace kept assuring Binah that it was only the extended Harrison clan, but Binah couldn't quite believe that. She counted at least twelve adults and many, many more children. Are all American families this big? she wondered.

Although there were a lot of them, Grace's family couldn't have been any nicer to Binah. One after another, the adults gave her huge hugs and said how happy they were to meet her. The children shyly gave her kisses and hugs and also said they were delighted to make her acquaintance. At least, that's what Binah thought they were saying. She'd heard an American accent before, but never one from the South. It was going to take some getting used to!

The second thing Binah noticed, when they had finally left the airport, was the heat. She and the London Harrisons had left England on a gray, foggy, and cool morning. Here in Atlanta the sun blazed high in the sky (although it was midafternoon), and the moist heat felt like a damp towel on Binah's body. As they walked through the parking garage, Binah peeled off the cardigan she'd worn on the plane. Her tummy was still doing flip-flops. Now her head was starting to ache because of the heat, and she was having a hard time keeping track of the conversations around her.

When they were all packed into the various cars that had come to collect them, Binah was very relieved to find herself sitting next to Grace. At least her voice was familiar!

"We're so happy that y'all could come along, Binah!" Grace's Aunt Teeny was saying. "We're always telling Grace to bring her friends, aren't we, Grace?"

"Yes, ma'am," Grace dutifully replied. Binah looked at her friend in amazement. Where had that "ma'am" come from? In all the years that Binah had known Grace, she'd never heard her utter that word!

"Thank you very much for having me," Binah said politely. "I am so looking forward to getting to know you and Atlanta." Binah had rehearsed that speech on the plane.

"Aren't you the sweetest thing?!" Aunt Teeny gushed. "We hope y'all will have a great time. We know that y'all must be tired, but we've got all kinds of things planned. Two weeks seems like a lot of time now, but we'll be back here dropping y'all off before we know it!" At that thought, Aunt Teeny looked sad.

"Let's not think about that now!" Uncle Howard urged from the driver's seat. "How do y'all feel about baseball?"

Grace laughed. "I love baseball, Uncle Howard!"

"Good," he answered. "Because we've got tickets to see the Atlanta Braves play tonight!"

"Brill! Ooops! I mean, fantastic!" Grace cried. "Isn't this great, Binah?"

"Yes," Binah agreed, although she really felt like taking a nap, and she hoped her ears would pop for good sometime very soon. "That sounds like fun."

The caravan of cars had made it to Aunt Teeny and Uncle Howard's house, where the English visitors were escorted inside. Binah and Grace were shown the room they were to share and given a few minutes to freshen up and unpack. Binah tried to

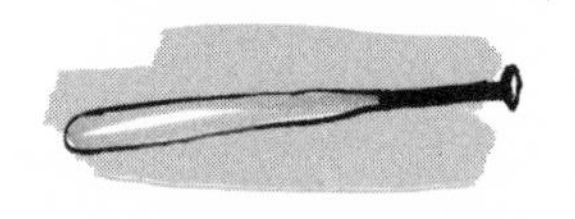

keep track of everyone she'd just met. She was sure of the fact that Aunt Teeny was Mr. Harrison's sister, but that was the only thing she was sure about!

"Don't worry about food, y'all," Uncle Howard had said. "We'll grab some food at the ballpark."

"Yummy!" Grace said. "I love hot dogs!"

"Me, too!" Matthew and Michael said in unison.

Binah said nothing because her stomach was still doing flip-flops. She was pooped after the flight and didn't understand how Grace and her brothers were still going strong. *I've got to toughen up!* she urged herself.

Which is how Binah found herself, several hours later, sitting at her first baseball game. Although it was early evening, it was still very warm and humid. "Muggy" is what Aunt Teeny called it. Around her, the crowd was going wild as the hometown Atlanta Braves beat the New York Mets.

"Let's go get some food," Uncle Howard said during the seventh-inning break.

"Grace and Binah, why don't you come with me?" he suggested. "You look like you could do with a good stretch!"

Binah hoped her confusion and slight boredom weren't obvious. She didn't want anyone to think that she wasn't having a good time. Clearly, this loud and chaotic event was a popular pastime in the U.S.!

Grace chattered about the players and their "stats" (*Whatever those are!* Binah thought) all the way to the concession stand.

"What are you girls in the mood for?" Uncle Howard asked.

"I'll have a hot dog!" Grace cried as Binah scanned the posted menu. Binah almost gasped out loud as she saw the prices. If she was reading the menu correctly, a hot dog and a soda would cost more than ten dollars.

Grace must have noticed something in her

friend's expression, because she quickly said, "Please order whatever you'd like, Binah."

Uncle Howard jumped in. "Yes, Binah. Y'all should order whatever looks good to you!"

Binah dug through her pockets, trying to find one of Nonna Rossi's twenty-dollar bills. At this rate, Binah worried, she'd be out of money before the end of the week!

But when Uncle Howard saw what she was doing, he quickly stopped her. "Now, Binah," he said kindly, "please remember that your money is no good here!"

"But—" Binah began.

"Absolutely not," Uncle Howard said firmly. "Y'all are our guests. Don't be reaching in your pocket again!"

Pa..
.pa
???

"Thank you," Binah said gratefully. "I'd love to try a hot dog, too."

"That's my girl!" Uncle Howard said.

"Good choice, Binah!" Grace said, giving her friend a hug.

Binah had to admit, after they got back to their seats, that the hot dog was quite tasty. Her stomach was still acting a little funny, the game still didn't interest her, and she was worried about running out of money; but she vowed to give herself some time. Binah sank back into her seat and tried to follow the action on the field below her. *After all,* she thought, *twenty-four hours ago I was sleeping in my own bed. I haven't even been here for a full day yet!*

No, No, YouR Money's No Good Here!

CHAPTER 6

Barba-What?!

Binah thought that a good night's sleep would do her a world of good, and she was right. She awoke the next day to find Grace smiling above her bed.

"How did you sleep, Binah?" Grace asked.

"Like the dead!" Binah laughed.

"You were out cold almost as soon as I turned off the light!" Grace teased.

"I know!" Binah said.

"I can understand why," Grace said. "You must have been nervous about meeting my family. Is everything okay so far?"

"Your family is wonderful, Grace!" Binah said. "They've been so welcoming."

"Good," Grace said. "I know that they love you. How could they not?"

"Thanks, Grace," Binah said.

When she and Grace had dressed and made their way downstairs, they found the kitchen a flurry of activity. In addition to Uncle Howard, Aunt Teeny, and the three little boy cousins who lived in the house, they found several other aunts, uncles, and cousins, along with Grace's parents and brothers.

"Good morning, sunshines!" Aunt Teeny sang out.

"We're glad you finally decided to join us," teased Mr. Harrison.

"Is this for us?" Grace asked, pointing at two plates piled high with eggs, bacon, biscuits, and some white, pasty stuff.

"It sure is!" Mrs. Harrison said. "Dig in!"

Grace attacked her plate as if she hadn't eaten in days. Binah was a little more cautious. "What is this stuff?" she asked Grace quietly, poking at the white, pasty glob on her plate.

"Grits!" Grace said. "They're yummy!"

Although her stomach was still acting funny,

Braves

Binah tried to eat as much as she could. The grits weren't half bad!

"What are today's plans?" Grace asked the adults.

"It's Sunday," Aunt Teeny said, "so it must be BBQ day!"

"Hooray!" said Grace, Matthew, and Michael together.

"Bee-bee what?" Binah asked.

"Binah," Grace began, "you haven't lived until you've tried my aunt's barbeque. Uncle Howard will light the grill, and Aunt Teeny will start cooking. She cooks everything: chicken, ribs, pork; you name it, we'll eat it!"

Binah couldn't imagine eating anything else today, but she just smiled and nodded. Soon she and Grace were put to work shucking corn and chopping vegetables for salads. While they worked, the kitchen got even noisier and more crowded as more and more family arrived.

Binah and Grace chattered away as they worked. When more cousins came by, however, Binah found herself becoming the center of attention for the younger crowd. Grace's cousins were friendly, but they were so hard to understand. Binah was sure they had a hard time understanding her, too,

but there were so many of them and only one of her. She had to keep asking Grace to interpret for her.

The interpreting went both ways: the cousins kept asking her to use her "English" words.

"Say 'truck'!" they asked.

It took Binah some time, but finally she realized what they wanted. "'Lorry,'" she answered, and they would giggle.

"Say 'elevator'!"

"'Lift'!"

Just when Binah thought they would never tire of the game, Aunt Teeny called them all out to the backyard. Uncle Howard had indeed lit the grill, and Aunt Teeny started cooking.

It seemed to Binah that the food never stopped coming. There were all sorts of meats, many that she had never seen before. There were tons of vegetables and salads and breads and biscuits. People

kept eating and eating. Binah did her best to keep up, but she wasn't used to eating like this.

Finally, she sat back in her chair, and one of the aunts (Binah was ashamed to admit that she couldn't remember the woman's name. Was it Gloria? Edna? She simply couldn't keep track of everyone!) asked if she wanted some tea.

Tea! *Just like at home!* Binah thought. "That would be lovely, thank you," she replied. Nothing would taste better than a nice, hot cup of English breakfast tea. That would surely help settle her stomach!

What the aunt brought, though, didn't look like any tea Binah had ever seen. It was a light brown liquid, but it was in a glass filled with ice cubes. More than that, there was a little green stalk sticking out. Binah didn't know if some salad had fallen into the glass and the aunt hadn't seen it. To be polite, she took the glass and took a sip.

"What is this?" she whispered to Grace as the aunt, smiling at her, walked away.

"It's iced tea, silly," Grace said.

"What's the green stuff?" Binah asked.

"That's mint," Grace said. "You don't eat it; it just flavors the drink. It's delicious!"

And although it wasn't at all what she was expecting, Binah had to admit that the cool drink was very refreshing. It was extremely sweet, and the mint gave it just the slightest sharpness. Binah felt the urge to pinch herself; here she was, far from home, drinking what was supposed to be tea. She thought about her papa and what he might be doing right now. It was the middle of the night in London, so he was probably fast asleep. Binah allowed herself a minute to think about her familiar house in London. She really missed Papa and Nonna Rossi. Grace's family was great, but everything was so strange here!

(home)...

CHAPTER 7

Home Is Where Your Heart Is

The time passed quickly for Binah and Grace. Each day brought a new adventure. They visited museums throughout the city. They day-tripped to other historical sites (who knew Atlanta had so much history!?). They traveled into the Buckhead section of the city to do some shopping. Binah was very careful with her money. Everywhere they went, Grace's parents or aunt or uncle offered to pay for anything for Grace and Binah. Grace always took them up on the offer (and why wouldn't she?!), but Binah felt too uncomfortable. She tried to use her own money as much as possible. She bought little souvenirs for Papa and Nonna Rossi, but not much more. She and Grace did pool their money to buy

...Hanging out with GANDHI

five T-shirts, one for each Rose, which said "I heart Atlanta!" Binah couldn't wait to see her friends and give them the shirts. She was having a great vacation; but as time passed, she felt more and more uneasy. They had been in Atlanta for nearly a week before she could identify the feeling: She was homesick! Binah had never been away from Papa for such a long time; it was no wonder that she missed him.

One afternoon as they strolled through the fashionable shops of Buckhead, Binah heard a familiar voice. She gasped, startling Grace, and turned quickly, looking for the man who was speaking.

"What is it, Binah? Are you okay?" Grace asked her.

"You look like a goose just walked over your grave!" Aunt Teeny said, concerned.

Binah found the speaker; it was just a man with a British accent . . . not her papa after all.

"Um, I'm fine," Binah said. "I feel sort of silly, though. I heard a familiar accent and thought it must be my father!"

"You have good ears, Binah!" Grace said. "I didn't even hear it!"

Aunt Teeny brushed her hand over Binah's hair.

"You're very used to our accents," she told Grace. "Binah is still getting used to us."

Binah smiled in gratitude.

Then Uncle Howard said, "And your dad is thousands of miles away, Binah!"

He didn't mean it unkindly, but Uncle Howard's words cut straight to Binah's heart. *Yes,* she thought. *He certainly is.*

The next day, events conspired to stir a little more sand into Binah's smoothie. They spent the entire day, from sunup to sundown (or at least that's how it felt to Binah) at an enormous amusement park, Six Flags. Binah had never seen anything like it! There were rides for little children, rides for adults, and rides for everyone in between.

"I want to find the biggest roller coaster in the

park!" Grace exclaimed as they studied a map of the park. "What do you say, Binah?"

Binah gulped. "I don't know," she said uncertainly. "Can I see it first?"

"Sure thing, Binah," one of the aunts said.

"If you don't like it, you can just sit down with me, honey," Aunt Teeny assured her.

Binah gulped again when she finally saw the monster coaster.

"I-I think I'll just wait here for you, Grace," she told her friend.

"Are you sure, Binah?" Grace asked.

"Oh, I'm very sure," Binah said.

"Do you mind if I go on?" Grace asked.

"Of course not, Grace!" Binah said. "I'll stay down here with Aunt Teeny. You can ride that thing as much as you want."

And so Grace and her brothers rode the monster coaster over and over. Binah first tried the Haunted House Ride with one of the younger cousins . . . and here comes some more sand for her smoothie! In her defense, though, Binah had never even seen anything like a Haunted House Ride.

"Don't worry," the little cousin Lally told her, "I've been on this one a million times. It's not scary; it's fun!"

So Binah was completely unprepared for the bloody, ghoulish creature that jumped out at them almost as soon as their little car had swung into the deserted mansion. Despite Lally's assurances, she couldn't help screaming. She couldn't help herself: every gory corpse, ghostly apparition, and headless body made her scream. Even when she could hear that she was the only rider screaming, Binah couldn't stop. She had never been so embarrassed in her life, but she simply couldn't stop.

At last the terrifying ride was over. As she stumbled out of the car, Binah looked for Grace or Aunt Teeny, but they were nowhere in sight.

"I'm sorry for screaming," she told Lally.

"That's okay," Lally said. "When I was little, I used to scream a lot, too. Why are all those people looking at us?"

Binah glanced around. The people getting off the ride behind them did seem to be looking at them closely. Glumly, Binah imagined that they wanted to see who had been making all that noise. She wondered if she should apologize to each of them.

Great! Binah thought. *I screamed more than little Lally did! At least I gave the other riders a funny story to tell their friends!*

"I'm hungry," Lally announced. "Can we get something to eat?"

"Sure," Binah said. She felt so guilty; she hoped she hadn't ruined Lally's ride. "What would you like?"

"Fried dough!" Lally announced cheerfully.

"Okay," Binah agreed. After all, she still had some money left, and how much could fried dough cost, anyway?

An awful lot, as it turned out. Buying fried dough for the two of them, along with two sodas, used up almost all of the money Binah had allotted for the next few days. *Criminy!* she thought. *I've got to be more careful from here on out. I don't want to completely run out of money.*

"What ride should we try next?" Lally asked. "How about the little Ferris wheel?"

"Sure," Binah answered. "That sounds like just my speed!" She looked around for other Harrisons, but there were none to be found. *I guess I should stick with Lally,* she thought. *At least we like the same rides!*

It was when she was at the very top of the baby Ferris wheel, holding hands with Lally, that Binah had the strangest feeling. The ride was stopped while more passengers loaded into the lower baskets. Binah's basket swayed gently at the top, and she had a clear view of the enormous park spread out around her. Everywhere she looked, families walked along, some hand in hand. Little kids were stuffing popcorn or cotton candy (another new food for Binah!) into their mouths. Everywhere she looked, Binah saw people talking, laughing, and having fun. That's when it hit her: she was all alone.

Oh sure, she was surrounded by Grace's large, friendly family. Everyone in Atlanta had been nothing but nice to her. But still. *I miss my family,* Binah thought. *My family is small, but it's all mine.*

She missed the noises Papa made while showering and shaving in the morning. These things were as familiar to her as the back of her own hand. *How bizarre that I feel so alone when I am around so many people!*

Binah tried to shake the loneliness, but it wouldn't go away.

"I'm being silly," she told herself. "I've got to be strong and make Papa proud. Grace's family is being so wonderful to me!" With that, Binah gave herself a little shake; and, by the time the ride started up again, she was smiling at Lally, seated next to her.

someone's hat
An adult screaming like a three-year-old
That's GRACE.

CHAPTER 8

Long-Distance Roses

The next day, Binah found it easier to keep her resolution, easier to keep the homesickness at bay. The whole Harrison clan spent the morning in Atlanta's Piedmont Park; they hiked trails, enjoyed scenery, played pickup football (Oops, soccer to you Americans!), and enjoyed the picnic lunch that the aunts had packed. Binah found herself laughing and joking with Grace's cousins. They still occasionally had trouble understanding each other, but not enough to stop the jokes from flying.

"How do you like Atlanta, Binah?" Uncle Howard asked for what seemed like the millionth time since the start of the vacation.

"I am having a lovely time," Binah answered. At first she thought that she was just being polite, but then she realized that she truly meant it. Atlanta was lovely, and the Harrisons were so warm and welcoming.

"We've only got a few days left!" Grace cried.

"Let's not talk about that, sugar," Aunt Teeny said. "I don't like thinking about y'all being gone. I'll be so lonely without you!"

"Oh, Aunt Teeny! Don't be sad!" Grace cried.

She gave her aunt a giant hug.

When Binah looked over at them, she was surprised to see Aunt Teeny motioning to her. She wanted to hug Binah, too! Without a second thought, Binah joined the hug. Then some of the smaller cousins ran over, and it became a whole group hug. Binah made herself relax and enjoy the crush of people.

I could get used to this! she thought.

When they finally arrived home early in the afternoon, some of the little cousins went down for a nap. As Grace and Binah headed to their room to relax before dinner, Uncle Howard called to them quietly.

"Come with me, ladies," he said.

Binah and Grace looked at each other. What was this all about?

Uncle Howard led the way to his office, a small room off the kitchen. He switched on his computer, and the machine hummed to life.

"I've got a surprise for y'all," he said.

"What is it, Uncle Howard?" Grace asked.

"Shush, honey, let me get this all set up," Uncle Howard answered.

As he typed on the keyboard, he began to speak. "I know that y'all have a tight group of friends back home. What do you call yourselves?

Binah + Grace + Aunt Teeny = Besties!

The Purple Lilacs? The Perfect Petunias?"

"The English Roses!" Grace and Binah said, laughing at Uncle Howard.

"Anyway," he continued, choosing to ignore their laughter, "I figured y'all must miss your friends, y'all being so close and all."

"I do miss the others a bit," Grace admitted. "But I'm so happy to have Binah here with me!" With that she gave Binah a big hug.

"How 'bout you, Binah?" Uncle Howard said. "Do you miss your friends?"

Binah hesitated. But surely Uncle Howard wouldn't ask if he didn't really want to know? "Yes," she finally said. "I love being here with your family and Grace, but I wonder what the other Roses are up to."

"What's this all about, Uncle Howard?" Grace asked again.

Uncle Howard kept typing, and soon Binah and Grace heard a sound like a phone ringing.

"Hello, hello?" Suddenly a very familiar voice filled the room, and Charlotte's smiling face filled the computer monitor.

"Surprise!" Charlotte and Uncle Howard said simultaneously.

"What?!" Binah and Grace said in unison.

"How is this happening?" Grace asked.

"We're talking over the computer hookup, silly!" Charlotte told them. "I'm in the living room at the villa."

"And we're in Uncle Howard's office!" Binah told her.

"How does this work?" Grace asked.

"I have no idea," Charlotte answered her. "And I don't really care. I'm so happy to see you two!"

"You can see us?" Binah asked, incredulous.

"Yes!" Charlotte exclaimed. "You can see me and I can see you and we can talk and I can get a Roses' fix!"

Grace and Binah turned to Uncle Howard in amazement. He laughed at their expressions and said, "I'll leave you ladies alone for a few minutes. I'm sure you have very important things to discuss."

"Thank you, Uncle Howard!" Binah said.

"Yes, thank you, Uncle Howard!" Charlotte's laughing voice filled the room.

As Uncle Howard left the room, he closed the door gently behind him; and the three friends

began to talk at once. Charlotte explained that Mrs. Harrison had called her mum earlier in the day and made all the arrangements. It was so much fun; it was almost as good as a regular chatfest under the tree in the park on Saturday morning.

What's more, when the three girls were finished (or as finished as a conversation ever is between the Roses), Uncle Howard had another surprise. After saying good-bye to Charlotte, Uncle Howard dialed another number, and soon the girls were talking to Nicole and Amy in Wales. Arrangements had been made with their camp counselors as well. Binah thought this might be the best surprise of her life . . . and her life had had lots of surprises!

Finally, Uncle Howard had

to interrupt the conversation between the four girls and announce that it was time to say good-bye.

"Good-bye!" Nicole and Amy cried.

"Good-bye!" Grace and Binah answered their friends.

"We'll see each other soon!" Nicole and Amy said.

"We can't wait!" Grace and Binah answered.

Then the screen went black.

"Oh, Uncle Howard!" Grace said. "That was brill!"

"Thank you so much, Uncle Howard," Binah said.

That night, Binah lay awake for a while. It had been so lovely to talk to and actually see her friends. She was thrilled that they were all having a good time. She was happy that she herself was having a good time. *Before we know it, we'll be home,* she thought drowsily. And at the mention of the word "home," Binah immediately felt a pang. That yucky, lurking feeling, that missing-Papa-and-her-own-room feeling reared its ugly head. Although she'd just had great, happy conversations with her closest friends in the world, she suddenly missed her papa terribly. She would have loved to have talked to him over the computer, too; but she and Papa didn't have a computer at home. And so Binah drifted off to sleep trying to remember the chatter and laughter of her friends but feeling sad and lonely instead.

CHAPTER 9

Bangers and Mash

BANGERS and MASH...

This time, the good night's sleep didn't quite do the trick for Binah.

Grace bounded out of bed the next morning. "Wasn't last night fun?" she asked Binah.

Binah forced herself to smile. "What is wrong with me?" she asked herself. "Yes, it was great!" she told her friend.

Throughout the morning, Binah found her thoughts drifting across the ocean to London. She wondered what her papa was doing. She wondered if he missed her as much as she missed him.

It was a rare rainy day in Atlanta and everyone was tired from their trip to the park the day before, so it was a quiet time in the Harrison house. Well,

as quiet as it can be with a whole house full of people. Grace's brothers found a football (I mean, soccer!) game on television; and, after lunch, Grace plopped down on the sofa with them.

"Come join us, Binah," Grace urged.

"We've got plenty of room!" Matthew said.

"No, that's okay, thank you," Binah answered. "I think I'll read in our room, Grace."

"Okay, Binah," Grace answered, already absorbed in the game. "Can you believe the pass Beckham just made?" she asked her brothers as Binah walked away.

Binah made her way down the hallway to their bedroom. She passed the kitchen, where bubbly Aunt Teeny was cooking something that smelled, Binah had to admit, delicious! She passed the little boys' room, where two were curled up in cribs, having an afternoon nap. She passed the living room, where Grace's parents were having a quiet conversation with Uncle Howard. Again, Binah had that strange feeling of being alone while surrounded by people.

Maybe I'm just overtired, she thought. *What would Nonna tell me right now?* she wondered. The answer came to Binah almost immediately. She could hear Nonna Rossi's voice clear as day. "What you need," the voice told Binah, "is a good nap. You're exhausted!"

"Okay, Nonna," Binah muttered to herself. And when she reached the room she shared with Grace, she stretched out on her bed and closed her eyes. Still thinking about Papa, Binah couldn't stop the tears that rolled silently down her cheeks. *I'll just have a good cry,* she thought. *Then I'll be right as rain.*

The skies cleared up a little while later, and Grace and her brothers decided to go into the backyard to kick around a soccer ball. Grace bounded into the room to retrieve her cleats and was surprised to find Binah asleep. Worse, when she looked closely at her friend, Grace was shocked to

see the tracks of tears on Binah's cheeks. Binah's pillow was damp to the touch.

"Hmm," Grace said quietly to herself. "This is wrong, plain wrong! I'm beginning to think that Binah is a very good actress. I wonder what Nicole, Amy, and Charlotte would have to say about this?"

When Binah woke several hours later, she was confused. Where was she? What was all that noise? It took her a minute to get her bearings. *Oh yes,* she thought, *Atlanta!* She padded her way into the kitchen, where dinner preparations were in full swing.

Aunt Teeny looked up to see Binah in the doorway. "Out, out!" she shooed. "Grace and the boys are in the backyard. Go and join them!"

"But," Binah said, "can I help you?"

"No," Aunt Teeny said immediately. "We're working on a surprise here. Out you go!"

"What kind of surprise?" Binah asked.

"Never you mind!" Aunt Teeny said. "Now, skedaddle!"

Binah wasn't sure how to "skedaddle," but she could tell that Aunt Teeny wanted her out of the room. She joined Grace, Michael, Matthew, and some of the little cousins in the backyard. They were playing some crazy game Matthew and

Michael had created. It involved soccer balls, hula hoops, and a garden hose. Binah joined in the fun, forgetting about the surprise in the kitchen and trying to forget about missing home.

Suddenly, a loud ringing came from the kitchen.

"What in the world is that?" Grace asked.

"It's just your aunt," Uncle Howard assured them, coming into the backyard. "She's trying her new dinner bell."

"Dinner bell?" asked Grace.

"Don't ask!" Uncle Howard urged them. "Let's just go eat!"

What do you think Grace and Binah found in the dining room once they'd dried off and brushed the grass out of their hair? I can assure you, it wasn't one of Aunt Teeny's famous BBQs. Nope (or 'No, sir' as they say in Atlanta)! Spread out over the table were all sorts of very familiar, very English foods. There were bangers and mash, scones, shepherd's pies, plates of baked beans on toast, cucumber sandwiches, mushy peas, and best of all . . . pots and pots of hot tea!

CHAPTER 10

One More Surprise

Michael and Matthew said, "Wow!"

Grace giggled.

Binah rubbed her eyes. She took a deep breath. It smelled just like home!

"Surprise!" the Atlanta Harrisons yelled together.

Aunt Teeny said, "We realized that y'all must miss your English food. Y'all have been such good

sports about eating BBQ and trying everything that Atlanta has to offer; we thought we'd cook you a traditional meal for a change!"

"Yum!" Grace squealed.

"Let's eat!" said Michael.

"Thank you so much!" Binah said.

"Grab some plates and dig in, everyone!" urged Uncle Howard.

Soon the only sounds in the dining room were

the clanking of silverware against plates and murmurs of "Please pass the peas." The cousins had a few questions for the London Harrisons about the food, which Grace and Binah were happy to answer.

"Where did you find all this stuff, Aunt Teeny?" Matthew asked.

"You know your aunt." Uncle Howard laughed. "There isn't a food out there that she can't find and cook with flair!"

Aunt Teeny smiled at her husband. "There's a lovely little English grocery store on Peachtree. I just popped over there and nosed around this afternoon. It was fun! And you

know," Aunt Teeny continued, "this was all Grace's idea."

"What?" Binah said, turning to look at Grace in surprise.

"Well," Grace said, "it was really Charlotte's brainchild."

"Charlotte?" Binah squeaked.

"Yes," Grace said. "While you were napping, she called me. She, Nicole, and Amy all noticed that you looked a little sad yesterday. We put our heads together and decided that you must be missing home."

"But I'm having a great time!" Binah protested.

"I know that," Grace said. "But we thought that a little reminder of home would make you feel better. Did it work?"

"Yes!" Binah said. "This all tastes delicious . . . and very, very familiar!"

"Now we'll know what to expect when we come and visit you!" one of the older cousins said.

"Ooooh! Could we?" another asked.

Grace and Binah looked at each other, then at Grace's parents. "Of course!" they said, laughing.

Binah finished off what seemed like her hundredth cup of tea. She gave a contented sigh. *What a wonderful world it is,* she thought, *with people like the Harrisons in it!*

And then, almost before they knew it, Binah and Grace (and Grace's family,

of course!) were winging their way back across the Atlantic. Binah had been very nervous about the flight home. When she explained to Aunt Teeny about her flip-floppy stomach, Aunt Teeny had said, "Why, sugar, I wish you'd told me. I know just the thing for motion sickness."

At the airport, Aunt Teeny slipped her a paper bag filled with, she explained, candied ginger. "Just chew on some of this when the plane takes off and lands, and your stomach will feel just perfect."

O.K. this dotted line
Represents an IN<u>STANT</u>.

Their flight was smooth and easy, and the candied ginger was yummy. Binah was very relieved to learn that Aunt Teeny knew exactly what she was talking about. Binah was coming to believe that Aunt Teeny always knew what she was talking about!

When their plane had landed and they were making their way through the airport, Grace turned to Binah and said, “It was so wonderful to have you along, Binah. I’ve never had so much fun in Atlanta before.”

“Thank you, Grace,” Binah said. “I love your family!”

“I see another family you love!” cried Grace. “Look over there!”

Baggage claim
ARRIVALS...

Binah followed Grace's pointing finger and saw a face she'd been looking for for days: Papa! And right next to Papa, holding tightly to his hand, was Miss Fluffernutter. Binah dropped her suitcase and ran to Papa; he and Miss Fluffernutter took turns squeezing her, kissing her, and hugging her. Nearby, the Harrisons patiently waited with their bags.

"Papa!" Binah cried. "I am so happy to see you!"

"Me, too, precious!" said Mr. Rossi.

"Me, three!" said Miss Fluffernutter. "Selfishly, it's been wonderful to have your father all to myself these past weeks. We've done lots of fun and interesting things, but half the time I think his mind was in Atlanta with you!" Binah could tell that Miss Fluffernutter was not angry; she'd missed Binah, too!

Papa nodded sheepishly. "It's true," he said. "I've missed you terribly. But how was your trip?"

"Oh, Papa!" Binah said, looking from his so-familiar face to Miss Fluffernutter's excited smile to Grace's lovable grin. "My adventure in America was a dream come true!"

And you know what? She meant it!

The End

Previous Books by Madonna

PICTURE BOOKS:

The English Roses

Mr. Peabody's Apples

Yakov and the Seven Thieves

The Adventures of Abdi

Lotsa de Casha

The English Roses: Too Good To Be True

CHAPTER BOOKS:

Friends For Life!

Good-Bye, Grace?

The New Girl

A Rose by Any Other Name

Big-Sister Blues

Being Binah

Hooray for the Holidays!

A Perfect Pair

Runway Rose

Ready, Set, Vote!

COMING SOON:

Catch the Bouquet

MADONNA RITCHIE was born in Bay City, Michigan, and now lives in New York with her children, Lola, Rocco, and David. She has recorded 18 albums and appeared in 18 movies. This is the eleventh in her series of chapter books. She has also written six picture books for children, starting with the international bestseller *The English Roses*, which was released in 40 languages and more than 100 countries.

JEFFREY FULVIMARI was born in Akron, Ohio. He started coloring when he was two, and has never stopped. Soon after graduating from The Cooper Union in New York City, he began drawing for magazines and television commercials around the globe. He currently lives in a log cabin in upstate New York, and is happiest when surrounded by stacks of paper and magic markers.

A NOTE ON THE TYPE:

This book is set in Mazarin, a "humanist" typeface designed by Jonathan Hoefler. Mazarin is a revival of the typeface of Nicolas Jenson, the fifteenth-century typefounder who created one of the first roman printing types.